# HOPSCOTCH

*OKUHLE ESETHU*

**OE PUBLICATIONS**

First published in South Africa in 2025 by

**OE Publications**

<u>Disclaimer\*\*</u>

This is a work of fiction.

Names, characters, places, and incidents are either the
product of the author's imagination or used fictitiously.
Any resemblance to actual persons, living or dead, or
actual events is purely coincidental.

ISBN: 978-1-0370-2185-5

For more information visit: www.oepublications.com

*too naïve, too hurt, too desperate to understand how love holds*
*a woman; she hopscotches from abuse to deadly lust.*

# CHAPTER ONE

*HOPSCOTCH*

Empty bottles of alcohol were strewn across MaBetty's yard, their contents long since drained. Plastic tables and chairs that had once been artfully arranged now lay scattered and overturned. The youth of Jabavu had a knack for squandering their prime days, and they had outdone themselves once again that night. The amaPiano, Maskandi, and Gqom music that blasted from the loud sound system, drowning the soberness and dreams of the young and misguided souls, along with the greedily consumed alcohol, was abruptly turned off.

The vulgar MaBetty chased away her inebriated patrons, who stumbled and struggled to leave even though the tavern had closed. Outside the tavern, the vile laughter of rowdy and naïve girls echoed through the sleeping streets as older men with sagging pot bellies dragged them towards their cars. The men expected repayment for the "kindness" they had shown the girls throughout the night—kindness in the form of the excessive alcohol the girls could not afford, and repayment in the form of the bliss they anticipated finding under their panties.

Though some girls went off to be with boys their own age, only a select few did so. They all reeked of breast milk, too young to be out on the streets, drunk, at that hour.

Most were still in high school, their bodies—breasts, buttocks, and curves—still developing.

MaBetty bore witness to this obscenity and the deterioration of the youth of Jabavu yet did nothing about it. Her sense and conscience had been numbed by the profits she made every weekend.

"A woman has to survive any way she can, even if it means being the host of the devil's den and selling the souls of the youth," she often rationalised.

Before her tavern became a den where predatory men preyed on naïve girls, she survived on the profits from older women who frequented the tavern to escape their own burdens and numb the endless pain weighing on their hearts, and older men who gathered to forget their problems and drown their shame. The men visited her tavern to avoid confronting the ghosts of their unfulfilled dreams, caused by the oppressive system, and their eroded youthfulness.

Her current patrons would eventually tell stories similar to those of the old-timers, as history repeated itself. This was a lineage trapped in an endless loop perpetuated by alcoholism. She knew this all too well…

\*\*\*

Intoxicated Zonke stumbled, arms wrapped around her boyfriend, Vusi, as they made their way back to his place. Her feet dragged across the uneven pavement, the world spinning slightly as she leaned heavily on him for support. By then, they had been dating for about three years, ever since Zonke was in grade eight. They exchanged brief, then passionate kisses as they walked, with Zonke half-conscious, collapsing onto his shoulder every few steps. The sedative effect of the alcohol fuelled their slowly rekindling passion, turning it into an aggressive thirst and hunger for each other, until they finally made it home, where Zonke passed out.

\*\*\*

The sun was shining brightly outside when Zonke finally blinked her tired eyes, her head heavy and pounding with a hangover. She stretched her left arm, feeling for Vusi, but her hand only met the softness of the mattress.

*Of course, he is already at work*, she thought to herself.

She flung the blankets open, her teardrop-shaped, pointed breasts swaying slightly as she sat up. Looking down at them, she realised she did not remember taking off her top. As she got out of bed, she noticed she had slept bare, with no recollection of stripping off her clothes, including her underwear. Her eyes shifted to the chair across from the bed, where her clothes were neatly folded and placed. Vusi had stripped her naked while she was passed out, then carefully folded her clothes and placed them on the chair. That was what he always did after they had sex—he made her sleep naked, with or without her knowing, wanting to feel her warm body against his sweaty skin. The meticulous folding of her clothes afterward was a subtle manifestation of his obsessive and controlling personality.

*Our spark must have been rekindled last night,* Zonke thought to herself as she looked at her clothes, a shy smile creeping onto her face.

But she did not remember having sex. The only thing she could recall was their shared passion at MaBetty's tavern—the endless kisses and teasing touches as she sat on his lap, both of them lost in their indulgence. Even that memory was hazy; she had drunk more than she could handle before the sun had set.

Although she could not recall their night of passion, as evidenced by her nakedness and the folded clothes in the morning, she was nonetheless pleased that her body had been a source of pleasure for him. She believed her body belonged to him since they were a couple. This was a belief she had internalised growing up—that a man owns a woman's body if they are together.

Zonke moved to Vusi's wardrobe to find a baggy t-shirt to wear. She winced in pain as she lifted her arms to put it on, her back stinging and her entire body aching. She slid her left hand over her shoulder to feel the part of her back that was most painful. The sting again!

She approached a freestanding mirror in the bedroom, stood with her back to it, and turned her head to examine the source of the soreness:

 A dark bruise stared back at her.

***

The sun was setting over the corrugated houses of Jabavu when Vusi returned home from work. The loud scrape of his steel door as he opened it startled Zonke from her sleep. She had unintentionally spent her Monday afternoon sleeping. After examining her aching back, she took some painkillers and dozed off, hoping to ease the pain. As she slept, her mind hopscotched from one ancient memory to another, tumbling through countless more. She woke up a few times between naps, only to drift off again. During those brief moments when her heavy eyes fluttered open, she thought about going home but could not bring herself to be around her stepfather, especially in her mother's absence. The thought of being with him without her mother always triggered a deeply ingrained and unsettling memory—one that kept her away from home most of the time. This memory stirred up intense aversion towards her stepfather. She recalled the morning she had returned home after spending the night at Vusi's place, struggling to suppress her nausea, tears, and overwhelming emotions upon encountering a disturbing sight when she opened the door. As she entered the house, her ears and eyes were drawn to the sounds of lustful moans coming from the lounge, where her stepfather shared a moment of passion with *another woman* on her mother's couch. At least, that was what she thought until her gaze shifted to the floor, where his clothes were scattered alongside a girl's school uniform. The pair—a grown and married man and a schoolgirl—had been so absorbed in their sordid act that they did not hear Zonke walking in on them and leaving, distraught.

Zonke kept her stepfather's obscenity to herself, gradually spending less time at home to avoid him. When she was not at school, she was either at Vusi's place—by herself or with him—or out with her friends. Her habit of not sleeping at home developed slowly, but it bred disappointment and endless rants from her mother all the same. The more Zizipho, Zonke's mother, yelled at and argued with her about dating a man eight years older and committing her life and future to him, the more she drove her naïve daughter away, pushing her further into the predator's embrace. Zizipho saw Vusi as nothing more than a predator with an erected penis to dangle between the thighs of unripe girls like her daughter, preying on their innocence and tainting their purity.

When Zizipho realised that her rants were driving a wedge between herself and her daughter, she kept her thoughts about Vusi to herself and retreated into mournful silence. She allowed her misguided daughter to follow her own path but silently prayed for her to see the truth, to return home, and to rediscover herself before it was too late, before her youth was entirely squandered.

With Zizipho's silence and the absence of her rants and judgment, Zonke fully embraced her newfound freedom. The nights spent at Vusi's place extended into weeks, leading to personal neglect and abandonment of her future, dreams, and schoolwork. Vusi moulded her into a docile and uninitiated housewife.


"Mamas," Vusi greeted with a smile as he struggled to close the door.

"You are back," Zonke mumbled, sitting up on the bed.

He walked over and sat beside her, leaning forward to kiss her on the cheek. Zonke winced as his hand wrapped around her back.

"What's wrong?" he asked, pulling away slightly, his eyes scanning her face for an answer.

"Eish! I don't know, I don't know," she said, touching her back. "My body is sore, and I have this bruise on my back." She lifted the baggy t-shirt up to show him.

His face contorted as if mirroring her grimace.

He said nothing.

"I don't even remember how I got it," she added, her eyes searching his for some kind of explanation.

Vusi sighed, rubbing his chin. "You were so drunk last night, maybe you fell. You know how wild you get." He forced a laugh, hoping to lighten the mood.

Zonke dropped the shirt back down, staring at the floor. His words did not sit right, but she could not deny that her memory of the previous night was a complete blur.

"Well, just rest," he added, wrapping an arm around her shoulders. "You will be fine."

She nodded, though uncertainty clouded her thoughts.

While Zonke struggled to piece together the events of the previous night, Vusi's mind effortlessly sprinted back to the truth. She could not remember how she got the bruise, but the memory of it was seared vividly into his haunted mind. Now that he was sober, the memory of his act of cruelty assaulted his spirit. His mind replayed the scene of him violently stripping her naked after repeatedly punching her back then throwing her against the wall. Her unconscious body slid down the wall to the floor, where she lay bare and bloodied, though her face remained unscathed. Whether sober or drunk, Vusi was always deliberate in unleashing his fists of fury, fuelled by his work worries and fragile masculinity. He never struck her face during his bouts of brutality. That night, he did not touch her sexually as he usually did when she blacked out. Instead, he folded her clothes neatly and placed them on the chair as she lay unconscious on the floor. Then, he stepped outside to smoke a cigarette. When he returned, he picked her up and tucked her into bed, lying down beside her bruised and bare body.

The next morning, he woke up an hour earlier for work to clean up the blood and erase any remnants of his abuse, actions concealed in the shadows. Now, as she began to ask questions, those shadows threatened to expose him, haunting his inner world. Shame crept in, but he quickly swept it away, justifying his actions by reminding himself of his anger and inability to contain his rage. He reminded himself of what had triggered his rage—feeling burdened by family responsibilities, frustrated by Zonke spending more time at his place than at her home, and angered by her being drunk as a skunk, acting foolish at the tavern. It was all too much for him. Unrecognisable anger had welled up inside him, but the previous night was a moment of misdirection in a fog of drunken thoughts and emotions. The man he was yesterday was not the man now sitting next to her. He looked at her face and swore to himself that he would never lose control like that again. His spiralling thoughts, laced with shame and unspoken apologies, were interrupted by the warmth of Zonke's voice.

"Vusi, I love you. Thank you for always making me feel safe," she said softly.

# CHAPTER TWO

*THE END*

*It is over! I am done with him! I have said this countless times before and still went back to him, but this time I mean it. I am done with Vusumuzi Gumede!* Zonke affirmed to herself as she leaned her head against the bus window, looking out at the passing landscape. Everything behind her seeming to fade as she moved forward. She had finally summoned up the courage to do it—to end things with Vusi and get as far away from him as possible. It took her years to finally see through his façade and admit that she was trapped in an unhealthy relationship. She had been groomed and subjected to abuse—mentally, emotionally, physically, and sexually. But she was not to blame for her situation; she was the victim—a teenager still finding herself, trying to navigate a cruel world filled with predators. Vusi eventually proved to be exactly what Zizipho had warned he was. His monstrosity revealed itself slowly, starting with doses of impatience and irritability, which grew into frightening outbursts that silenced Zonke into submission.

"Predators can't pretend forever," Zizipho had said.

The outbursts manifested as beatings, insults, and demeaning remarks. At first, Zonke convinced herself that the brutality she endured stemmed from the financial pressures he faced. This was his justification whenever he apologised to her after violently attacking her. Zonke sympathised with him, feeling that her presence at his place was an added burden. To her, the abuse from Vusi was more bearable than being home with her stepfather. However, over time, it became evident that the abuse was a reflection of Vusi's deeper, unresolved issues. It was a shadow of his past. His first act of violence towards a woman had occurred years before he met Zonke, directed at his ex-girlfriend, Angela. In a moment of panic and uncontrollable anger, he had beaten her into a coma when she broke the news of her pregnancy to him. When he heard the words, "I am pregnant," fear crept in and crippled him internally. In his terror, he struck her. After the first slap, he tripped her, and when she fell, he began kicking and stomping on her body with the force and fury of a raging bull. When he had exhausted his energy and looked down at her, she lay still and silent, not the kind of silence that masked suffering and agony, but the kind that hinted at death. In that instant, guilt took over Vusi, wrenching his heart and filling it with fear—the same fear he had felt as a boy, witnessing his father being beaten and necklaced by a furious, unforgiving community. His father had been accused of being a leader of one of the gangs that terrorised the neighbourhood. When the rumour circulated and twisted into a perceived truth, the community armed themselves with sjamboks, spades, knives, and other weapons, ready to destroy what they believed was the root of Jabavu's decay. In Vusi's world, violence was transmitted from generation to generation, like a disease spreading through a family tree in various forms.

The shackles of Vusi's fragile masculinity fell off like old paint being scraped from a wall when he realised what he had done. For a moment, he was frozen, his mind racing. *Have I killed her?* The thought of jail terrified him, but even more frightening was the reality of what he had become. He fell down to his knees next to Angela's body, trembling. Shaking her proved futile. Tears welled up in his eyes as his façade of bravery and hyper-masculinity crumbled. In that moment, all that remained in his shack was a battered girl and a frightened little boy hiding behind a false sense of manhood.

After six days in a coma, Angela finally stirred, her consciousness slowly returning from the abyss that Vusi had violently cast her into. He had frantically called an ambulance when the gravity of his actions sank in. As she awoke to a world overshadowed by rage and fear, her eyes revealed the torment and anger that had been brewing beneath the surface—a painful reminder of the savagery she had endured. The devastating news of her baby's death brought a fresh wave of grief and loss. It solidified Vusi's transformation from an abusive lover to a killer, a monster whose cruelty had irrevocably shattered her world.

Some women are forgiving and offer countless second chances to their abusers; Angela was not one of them. She had resolved to leave Vusi the moment he threw the first slap, and upon waking from the coma, she remained resolute in her decision. She never went an inch close to Vusi or anyone associated with him again, until one morning, more than four years after the incident, when she unexpectedly bumped into Zonke at a local clinic.

The two unacquainted young women, Zonke and Angela, sat side by side in silence on the cold, silver benches in the clinic's waiting area, each waiting to be called into the doctor's office.

"I am here for family planning, you?" Angela broke the silence, her voice soft and inviting.

"Pain," Zonke replied coldly, her tone shutting down the conversation Angela had hoped to ignite.

Angela glanced down at Zonke, noticing the hoodie pulled low over her head on such a bright, sunny morning. In that quick, curious look, she spotted the bruises on Zonke's hand and instantly understood what she meant by "pain," and why she wore a hoodie while the sun danced eagerly outside. The hoodie was not for warmth; it was a shield, hiding the bruises, the patches of shame that marked her body. *Was she in some kind of tavern fight? Was it a relative, a friend, or a lover who did this to her?* Angela thought to herself, feeling a deep pang of pity for Zonke. Still, she intended to mind her own business, as people in the township often do, even when a woman's life is in danger. But then Zonke switched on her cellphone, and Angela caught a glimpse of her wallpaper.

The anger Angela had tried to suppress over the years surged within her as the image of Vusi, holding hands with Zonke, glared back at her. She knew that face all too well, and in that moment, she was convinced the likelihood of Zonke being in the clinic, in pain, covered by a hoodie on a sunny morning, because of him, was high. *Abusers do not change*, she thought bitterly, her eyes welling with tears. A part of her wanted to grab Zonke and shake her, to demand how long she had been enduring his cruelty and abuse. But she choked on her tears, swallowed by the emotions erupting inside her. Unable to bear the burden of it all, she stormed out of the clinic, sobbing like someone who had just lost a loved one.

It was only a few days after her triggering encounter with Zonke that Angela decided to confront Vusi. She knew exactly where to find him on Sundays—MaBetty's tavern. She stormed inside, her heart pounding with fury, ready to confront the brute she had once loved but now venomously loathed.

"You bastard!" she hurled her first insult, her eyes fixed on her target.

Vusi had his arm wrapped around Zonke's waist as she sat on his lap, but when he spotted Angela, he quickly pushed Zonke aside and stood up, surprise and fear etching his features.

"You did it again! You abusive bastard! You are still the monster I left behind. I saw her. I saw what you did to her!" She pointed at Zonke, her concern evident.

The usually raucous crowd in the tavern fell into a curious silence, becoming spectators of the unfolding drama. MaBetty emerged from behind the bar, arms crossed, her eyes narrowed on the confrontation between Vusi and his former lover.

"Angela! What the hell is wrong with you?" Vusi shouted, attempting to sound authoritative as he closed the distance between them and tried to pull her aside.

"You beat her up, don't you?" Angela yelled, straining against Vusi's grip.

She pulled away but stood her ground, facing him.

"Was it not enough when you shattered my life? Did you not learn when you killed your own blood?" Her temper flared with each word, her rage echoing through the air.

The drunk spectators gasped in shock at the revelation of Vusi's viciousness, hearing about it for the first time after believing him to be a decent and loving man—a façade he had always maintained in public. Some people clapped their hands together and shook their heads in disbelief, as if witnessing a scene from a dramatic soap opera. Shame and guilt pierced Vusi's heart.

The entire time, Zonke stood there, grappling with a sense of familiarity about the girl. It only clicked when Vusi called out her name, and she remembered hearing it at the clinic when she registered at reception. Zonke felt her heart sink into a swamp of melancholy and deep disappointment as she absorbed Angela's impassioned outburst. Each word unsettled her, stirring a turbulent mix of shame and sorrow within.

"You are an abuser and a murderer!" Angela spat, her voice thick with fury, before storming out of the tavern. The crowd was left to gossip about the shocking revelation of Vusi's dark truth, the heaviness of the accusations hanging in the air. Vusi slowly turned to face Zonke, tears streaming down his cheeks. She met his gaze with a loathsome expression, her own tears falling as she trembled, feeling trapped in a prison of emotion.

The contempt in her eyes pierced him, and he could not bring himself to hold her gaze or move towards her. Lowering his head, he turned and walked out of the tavern, the burden of his shame pressing on his shoulders and dragging down his steps. Even with his back to everyone, he could still feel their judgemental stares burning into his skin.

And that was the last time Zonke ever saw Vusi.

# CHAPTER THREE

## TAVERN TALK

There are two types of township talk: polite talk and tavern talk. The truth lies somewhere in between.

The polite talk around Jabavu was that Zonke had fled the township out of fear; she had run away because of Vusi, from Vusi, who hid from the world during the day and tormented her at night. "Poor girl," they sympathised.

The tavern talk tarnished Zonke's reputation, circulating rumours that speculated she had avenged herself for all the years of abuse—first delivered in secret while she slept and then blatantly inflicted while she looked at him with pleading, desperate eyes—and killed Vusi shortly after she left the tavern pale and numb, having learned of his history with Angela. That, they said, was why no one had seen Vusi since that confrontation.

Despite the township talk, Zonke felt a surge of pride in finally leaving her connection to Vusi behind in Jabavu and reclaiming her power. She packed everything she owned into her suitcase—her clothes, books, important documents, and, unintentionally, her trauma too. She looked forward to a fresh start, yet parts of her past self lingered. The parts she believed defined her. The parts that reminded her of her background. The parts that overshadowed her dreams and goals. The parts that hindered her healing. The parts that attracted predators. The parts that made her accept abusive treatment. The parts that made her hate herself. The parts of herself that she still needed to grieve and forgive…

She did not feel too enthusiastic as the bus carried her to a new and unfamiliar destination. Yet, a part of her knew this was what she needed, what her empty soul and wounded heart needed. There was a faint sense of rebirth stirring within her, as if a tiny spark had been kindled deep inside, and she silently prayed for the strength and courage to make it burn brighter. *With great loss comes abundant blessings and wisdom,* she reminded herself, feeling like a shy caterpillar slowly transforming into a butterfly.

In front of her, an old couple sat in quiet intimacy, their bodies subtly intertwined as if they had long ago learned the art of being together. Zonke watched them for a while, noticing the way the husband gently stroked his wife's hair as she rested her head on his shoulder. They seemed truly in love, the kind of lovers who spoke a language that required no words. Envy struck Zonke as she admired the woman's calm comfort, but it was quickly followed by a question: *Had she ever endured abuse from her seemingly gentle husband? The way her mother had with her stepfather? The way she had with Vusi?*

She felt her thoughts spiralling, pulling her back into a place she no longer wished to revisit, a place she was determined to leave behind. With a deep breath, she shifted her focus outside the window, where the sun was setting, making room for the encroaching night. She laid her head back and closed her eyes, inviting sleep for the long journey ahead.

*\*\*\**

After more than fifteen hours on the road, with a few pit stops along the way, the bus finally came to a halt at the Civic Centre Intercity Bus Station in Cape Town. Zonke had slept through most of the journey, using sleep as a refuge from the painful memories that resurfaced whenever she was awake. As the driver opened the door, passengers began to disembark, retrieving their lighter belongings from the overhead compartments before stepping off the bus. They gathered outside, waiting for the driver to unlock the large, underbelly compartment where their heavier luggage was stored. Zonke stood silently among them, her thoughts elsewhere. When her suitcase appeared, she collected it, gripping the handle tightly as she moved away from the terminal. Each step felt heavier than the last, as if the weight of her past clung to her just as her luggage did. As she approached the roadside, an unfamiliar voice called out her name. Startled, Zonke turned towards the sound and spotted an exuberant woman emerging from a sleek 2022 BMW M2. The woman hurried towards her with a beaming smile and outstretched arms, radiating warmth and excitement. Zonke instantly recognised her cousin, Rethabile, the moment she saw her radiant face. Retha unmistakably carried the features of their maternal side, resembling a younger version of Zizipho's sister, Mawande. The warmth in Rethabile's eyes and her bright smile confirmed her identity. Zonke could not help but return the smile, feeling a flicker of connection amidst her inner turmoil. Once Retha crossed to the other side of the road, she embraced Zonke with welcoming love. Though they had never met or spoken before, they knew of each other through the stories shared by their mothers. Retha had seen a picture of Zonke before, but Zonke never concerned herself with those things. She never imagined she would meet Retha, let alone need her help in rewriting a chapter of her life. Yet, as she stood there, Zonke felt a deep sense of gratitude for having a cousin who would take her in when she desperately needed to escape her past. It was Zizipho who had asked Retha to help Zonke find her feet after Zonke finally humbled herself and reached out for help. She had told her mother she needed to leave Jabavu, to start afresh, and explore a new world, one where she could redefine herself. Zizipho, who had kept in close contact with Retha over the years, made the request, and Retha had agreed without hesitation. Twelve years older than Zonke, Retha's poise and success were evident in the way she carried herself, exuding confidence with each step.

"Welcome to Cape Town, cuzz!" Retha exclaimed as they embraced, her voice vibrant and full of energy.

They broke the hug, and Retha gestured towards the car, leading Zonke in its direction. A handsome man sitting behind the steering wheel stepped out and extended his hand to greet her. After exchanging polite greetings, he took her bags and effortlessly loaded them into the car. Zonke studied his physique, finding him far more attractive than Vusi had ever been. He exuded an aura of gentleness she had never encountered in men—a kind of gentleness that often intimidated girls like her. She felt she could have called him "beautiful" instead of "handsome," a term her friends from Jabavu used for Vusi, who possessed a pronounced masculine presence with his tall, broad-shouldered, and muscular frame. Zonke had been obsessed with how Vusi looked. Mostly, she loved his eyes. She had always found them deep and expressive, the kind of eyes that could easily capture her attention and draw her in. She often lost herself in their gaze, believing they held unspoken emotions. His deep dimples, which appeared on his brown cheeks whenever he smiled, only added to his charm, making him even more irresistible to her. She missed him, she realised as she jumped into the backseat of the car. His visage was vivid in her mind and looked like it would take forever to fade. Retha was already seated in the front passenger seat when the attractive man with a gentle demeanour, who had helped Zonke store her bags in the boot, jumped into the driver's seat. His movement interrupted Zonke's mental replay of Vusi's face and body, snapping her back to the present moment.

"So, babe, this is my cousin, Zonke. Cuzz, this is my partner, Thomas," Retha formally introduced them as her boyfriend ignited the engine. Zonke nodded politely from the backseat, still processing the whirlwind of new faces and emotions.

"Nice to meet you," Thomas said, his tone genuine, before driving off.

As they drove into the estate, Zonke felt overwhelmingly out of place, taking in the kind of life her cousin lived. The world she came from and the one she was now entering were stark contrasts. Retha's life seemed almost fictional to her, a far cry from everything she had known. The estate looked immaculate and serene, making her feel like an intruder who might pollute its purity. Unlike in Jabavu, there were no heaps of rubbish dumped by the roadside, and no street corners occupied by dagga-smoking young men loitering and catcalling passersby. There were no makeshift shacks crowding already congested RDP houses. Instead, this place was lined with well-designed apartment buildings, neatly paved walkways, and a boom gate controlling who came in and out. Retha's world of luxury made Zonke uneasy after having lived a humble life in the slums of Jabavu. The stark contrast between their backgrounds drove home the reality that she was no longer in Jabavu, within Vusi's vicinity. She was now far from everything she had known. She had never considered herself poor until that moment; before then, she had nothing to compare her life in Jabavu to. This was a complete rewrite of her life's script. Once they stepped inside the apartment, Retha led Zonke to a glass sliding door that opened onto a balcony with a breathtaking view of the ocean. As Zonke stepped outside, a feeling of nervous excitement replaced all other emotions, her heart racing at the sight before her. The vast expanse of water shimmered under the sun, a brilliant blue stretching endlessly to the horizon. She stood mesmerised, the sheer beauty of the scene overwhelming her. In that moment, she felt a profound sense of wonder and disbelief at how different this life was from everything she had ever known. The sound of the waves crashing against the shore echoed in her ears, a soothing reminder that she was finally stepping into a new chapter of her life. In her eighteen years, Zonke had never ventured beyond Jabavu. She had spent her entire life in that small slum, hardly daring to dream of a life outside its confines. Jabavu Secondary School was just a short walk away and nearby was a modest shopping centre where she could buy groceries, basic clothing options, and other necessities. Her world had revolved around Vusi, who offered her love and affection, MaBetty's Tavern, a spot for recreation and entertainment, and the familiar streets of Jabavu where she and her friends would roam, trading gossip and laughter. That existence had once felt complete, but now, as she stood on the balcony gazing at the endless ocean, her perspective began to shift. She realised how much her former surroundings had constrained her ambitions and how vast the possibilities were beyond the narrow confines of her upbringing. The ocean's shimmering horizon beckoned her to envision a future brimming with opportunity, far removed from the limitations she had always known. Her heart ached as she reflected on the magic and bliss she had missed, all because she had believed that life revolved solely around Vusi, the streets of Jabavu, and MaBetty's tavern. She mourned the life she had not lived, grieving for the opportunities and experiences that her narrow perspective had kept her from embracing. Her unfulfilled dreams unsettled her, making her acutely aware of the vibrant world waiting just beyond her reach.

# CHAPTER FOUR

*A DIFFERENT LIFE STORY*

Zonke quickly adapted to the world Retha had introduced her to. What once seemed like the bewildering complexities of a privileged life—fine dining, designer clothes, and polished social etiquette—soon became part of her new normal. The confusion and frustration she initially felt gave way to a sense of belonging as she learned to navigate this unfamiliar terrain. Through it all, Retha's warmth and support never wavered. Her gestures of love were sincere and patient, offering Zonke not only a place to stay but also a nurturing space to heal and grow. However, in Zonke's demeanour, Retha could trace the familiar signs of a girl still deeply in love with a rhythm that had broken her countless times. It manifested physically in the way she often hunched over, her shoulders slumped as if carrying an invisible burden, resembling a tired old woman. There was a heaviness to her posture, a visible reflection of the emotional scars she bore, as though she was bracing herself against the world, unwilling, or unable, to let go of the pain that had become so familiar.

"Cuzz, I've been observing you, you know?" Retha said one afternoon, her voice gentle but purposeful.

The words seemed to come out of nowhere, but she had spent a long time trying to articulate what she saw in the way Zonke carried herself—how her cousin presented herself to the world with a guarded, almost fragile demeanour.

"Studying me?" Zonke raised her eyebrow, wondering if this was the moment when the host grew weary of the guest's presence and began to subtly hint that they were becoming a burden.

"Yes, studying you, to understand how you ended up here and why you might be the way you are," Retha said gently, her eyes searching Zonke's face for understanding.

Zonke's heart tightened as she listened, uncertain where this was going.

"It's the way you walk," Retha continued, pausing to choose her words carefully. "I don't know how to say this without sounding harsh, but it's like you are carrying an invisible weight on your shoulders. You seem... unconfident and apologetic about your existence, almost like you are afraid to take up space, to be seen."

She glanced at Zonke, gauging her reaction. "You are here now, in a new place, with a chance to redefine yourself, but I can see that you are still holding back, as if the shadows of Jabavu are following you. I just want to understand what is keeping you from stepping fully into this new chapter of your life."

Zonke felt a sting of vulnerability. Retha's words were perceptive, touching on the insecurities she had not dared to voice. She looked away, swallowing hard, the truth of her own fear and self-doubt echoing in the silence between them. Retha gently pulled Zonke towards the fridge, urging her to look at their reflection in the polished surface of the stainless-steel door.

"Look at yourself, really look," she said softly, her tone both encouraging and firm. "You can tell a lot about a person from their posture and where their eyes are fixed when they walk," Retha explained, her gaze steady on Zonke's reflection.

As Zonke focused on her image, she noticed the subtle way her shoulders slumped and her back hunched over.

"Your posture and demeanour make it seem like you don't trust yourself enough to just be you," Retha continued.

"It's like you're trying to make yourself smaller by hunching like that."

Zonke glanced at her reflection, slowly starting to understand what Retha meant.

"See, a lady, a confident lady, walks like this," Retha stood tall, her back straight and shoulders pulled back, chest open. "That kind of posture makes you look confident and brave, sweetheart. But more than that, it makes you feel good about yourself."

Zonke watched her, noticing how Retha effortlessly filled the space around her, standing tall and unapologetic. As she looked on, something kindled within her, a flicker of confidence she had not known was there. It was still buried deep, a fragile seed that would take time and nurturing to fully bloom, but the spark had been lit.

That night, Zonke stood alone in front of the bedroom mirror, studying her posture with newfound curiosity, trying to straighten her spine and square her shoulders like Retha had shown her. While she gazed at her reflection, her mind hopscotched back to the last time she had stood in front of a mirror, scrutinising herself. The memories began to surface, some blurry and shadowed by time, but unmistakable in their heaviness. Her thoughts landed first on those mornings when she had woken up with bruises and cuts, assuming they were from drunken falls or brawls at the tavern, just as Vusi had told her. It was not until later that she realised they were the marks of assaults—violence inflicted while she was too intoxicated to defend herself. Slowly, the memories sharpened, and she remembered the times when she was fully conscious, the abuse no longer hidden behind the veil of blackouts but staring her down, raw and unfiltered. The recollections deepened her hatred for the reflection staring back at her. Unable to bear the sight any longer, she turned away and slipped into bed, seeking solace in the darkness. But instead of finding peace in sleep, her memories morphed into vivid dreams. She found herself reliving the past—when she first met Vusi, when he had still treated her with gentleness, then when he turned into a violent brute. Those memories flashed like scenes in a theatre, playing out in the depths of her mind, haunting yet familiar.

*Dressed in royal blue reflective safety overalls on his way home from work, Vusi had approached Zonke one evening as she strutted through the streets of Jabavu with her friends. She had already been infatuated with him before they even exchanged words. For weeks, she had noticed him watching her from afar, silently stalking her every move. It flattered her that a man as mature as Vusi seemed to have an interest in her. Her friends were quick to encourage her, saying that being with a man like him would elevate her from a girl to a woman. Together, they spent weeks scheming to create moments for the two to "bump" into each other, hoping for Vusi to finally approach her. Each day, they would wander a specific route in Jabavu at dusk, knowing that it was the path Vusi took on his way home from work. As he passed by, his eyes would lock on Zonke, claiming her with a deep, magnetic gaze that entranced her. His stare was filled with longing, each glance drawing her in deeper. She and her friends would giggle with excitement, like the little girls they still were, as they eagerly awaited his next move. Zonke and her friends had deemed him the finest suitor in the neighbourhood, and she eagerly anticipated the moment he would finally ask her out.*

When that moment came, it was not as romantic as she had imagined, but Vusi's charm still captivated her. He simply walked up to her and her friends, greeted them casually, then turned to Zonke, his desired woman, with a knowing smile.

"You know you are my woman, right?" he said confidently. "I'd like your company as I walk home this evening," he added, as if it were already decided.

Zonke, caught off guard, fixed her gaze to the ground in the shy manner girls often do in the presence of their suitor.

"If you don't mind," Vusi said softly, lifting her chin gently with his hand, forcing her to meet his eyes. She nodded, speechless, and without another word, she walked away with him.

In the days that followed, this became their routine— Zonke walking Vusi home. With each step they took side by side, her infatuation grew, and soon, she found herself longing for those stolen moments more than anything else...

When she woke up, she could not understand why her mind refused to let go. Even after so many months away from Jabavu, Vusi was still the first person she thought about each morning. His presence lingered, like a shadow that refused to fade. During the day, when she was left alone in the apartment—while Thomas and Retha were at work—memories of him kept her company. It was as if her mind sought comfort in the pain, hopscotching back to the past, allowing it to haunt her. At night, dreams of him returned, weaving themselves into her sleep, leaving her trapped in a cycle she no longer knew how to escape. *Perhaps doing something with my life will help me move forward*, she thought to herself, feeling worn out by the pull of memories from her painful past. And so, the seed of returning to school to finish her Matric was planted.

In the days that followed, Zonke tried to nurture the seed she had planted, hoping it would bloom into something that would bring her healing. First, though, she needed Retha's guidance.

"Retha, I need your help," she said on a breezy September evening as they prepared dinner together.

"Yes, I am listening," Retha replied, setting down the knife she was using to chop vegetables, her full attention now on Zonke.

"I want to register to go back to school next year. Can you help me?" Zonke asked, her voice tinged with nervousness and a hint of embarrassment. But Retha's response quickly melted away any unease, as she beamed with pride at her cousin's request. *Finally!* she thought. *Cuzz is moving on, trying to make something of her life, just like her mother had always hoped.*

"Of course! Yes! I will help you, cuzz," Retha said, embracing Zonke with joy and excitement. "Oh, I am so proud of you!" she exclaimed, pressing a kiss to Zonke's forehead.

Retha was brimming with enthusiasm over Zonke's decision to return to school. Zonke, on the other hand, found herself in a swirl of conflicting emotions. While she knew she should feel excited or happy about this new chapter, anxiety gnawed at her. Yet beneath that layer of apprehension, there was a spark of pride—a quiet acknowledgment that she was taking a step towards reclaiming her life and forging a better future.

# CHAPTER FIVE

*GENTLE LOVE*

Zonke felt overwhelmed by a wave of unexplainable emotions as she awaited the coming year to return to school and start pursuing her dreams. Retha had done everything in her power to help her find a school, but now her focus shifted to her own career, working towards a promotion at the law firm. This meant longer hours at the office and less time at home. Thomas did not mind Retha's sudden busyness; in fact, he admired it. He loved her ambition and determination. She was a dreamer, passionate and hardworking—the kind of woman he wanted by his side as they built their future together. He encouraged and supported her in every way he could. However, with Retha's increasing absence, Thomas found himself spending more time with Zonke. As the days passed, they began to connect on a deeper level, and an unexpected bond started to form between them. They bonded over shared hobbies. Thomas introduced Zonke to his fitness lifestyle. In the mornings, they would jog along the beach, attend yoga classes together, or hit the gym. At first, Zonke struggled to keep up, her body unused to the rigour. But Thomas was patient, guiding her gently and offering encouragement with every step. He moved at a pace that allowed her to adjust, making her feel supported rather than pressured. Over time, Zonke grew more comfortable, and their early morning routines became a comforting ritual for her, a space where she felt both challenged and cared for. In the evenings, they shared the meals they had prepared together, opening up to each other through intimate, soulful conversations that allowed them to explore one another's inner worlds. The gentleness that had once been a turnoff for her in men eventually became the very thing she cherished most about Thomas. For the first time in her life, she saw a man who not only embraced his softer side but thrived within it. Like Zonke, Thomas shed his initial biases as they grew closer. Though she appeared rough around the edges, he discovered her sincerity and tender-heartedness, revealing the beautiful soul within. He compared her to a rose, its sharp thorns contrasting with the delicate petals that exuded a heavenly scent. She was also a good listener, making him feel truly seen and heard for the first time in a long time. Zonke listened without judgement—he could tell from the way she looked at him whenever he opened up to her—and without hurrying to give him advice, the way Retha often did. He also enjoyed their small talk and playful banter. They spoke about the small yet meaningful things that held their lives together, like the weather when it ruined their plans, the characters in the movies they watched, the flavours of the meals they shared, and the beauty of the ocean that calmed their spirits. Life slowly became wonderfully simple with Zonke. In her presence, he could breathe, be in the moment, live, and just be.

*\*\*\**

It was a Thursday afternoon when Thomas and Retha had gone to work, and Zonke was alone in the apartment when Zizipho called, relaying news that blurred the line between Zonke's healing and hurting.

"I don't know how you will take this, but Vusi's mother was here last night," Zizipho began, her voice uncomfortable from the other end of the line. Zonke remained silent, bracing herself as her heart raced, waiting for her mother to confirm what she dreaded—that Vusi had returned to Jabavu.

"Vusi is no more," Zizipho said solemnly. Zonke inhaled sharply, the words triggering an avalanche of sadness within her. Although separated by many kilometres, Zizipho could sense the depth of the pain unfolding on the other end.

"No more? What do you mean, no more?" Zonke's voice quivered, her mind struggling to come to terms with the reality of the world she left behind.

"He was murdered, *m'tanami*," Zizipho's words hung in the air like a dark and heavy cloud.

There was a beat of silence, then she added, "It has been many months since he was killed. His body was only found a week ago, when some men were digging to put up shelter in that abandoned field behind your old school." Zizipho's voice was low, but heavy with sorrow.

Zonke felt her chest tighten as she absorbed the news of her old lover's demise. The shock left her numb, her mind reeling as memories of Vusi flooded in, now tainted by this new, unbearable reality.

"Okay, goodbye, Ma." Zonke's words barely made it past her lips before she hung up. Her body trembled under the heaviness of grief, and as the reality of the news settled in, she dropped to her knees, a guttural howl of pain escaping her as tears flowed uncontrollably.

She could hardly make sense of it all. The world suddenly felt lonelier than ever before. Vusi's existence might have unfolded away from her, or so she thought, when she left

Jabavu. But the idea that he was somewhere, still living, had kept a part of her alive too. In a strange way, it had given her hope—hope that someday the past could be rewritten. As long as they were both alive, anything was possible.

But now, he was gone. And she was alone. Forever.

The walls around her seemed to close in, suffocating her along with the flood of memories. Tears streamed down her face, soaking her skin as grief tore her apart. She collapsed onto the cold tiles, pressing her forehead against the floor, letting the pain, the rage, the regret consume her. The cold bit into her skin, but she welcomed it, as if it could dull the unbearable ache inside. She let the grief consume her.

***

Thomas was gripped by terror as he walked in and found Zonke's body lying motionless on the floor. His bag slipped from his shoulder as he rushed to her side, fearing she had fainted or worse. But as he drew closer, he felt the chill of her skin and saw her chest rising and falling slowly, a fragile rhythm of breath. She had fallen asleep there, lost in her sudden bereavement.

"Zee! Zee!" he whispered, shaking her gently.

She awakened slowly, the deep pang of grief still clinging to her heart. As her swollen, bloodshot eyes fluttered open, she was met with the concerned face of Thomas, his expression etched with worry. Fear settled in his chest like a stone as he looked into her eyes, seeing the agonising pain reflected back at him, a mirror of her sorrow.

"What's wrong, Zee?" he asked softly.

Zonke felt the tears well up again. "He is gone. He is gone," she murmured into the stillness, her voice breaking before she succumbed to deep, trembling sobs that echoed in the quiet room.

It took Thomas a long time to soothe Zonke's overwhelming grief. He held her close on the couch, brushing his hand along her back as if the gentle motion could somehow reach into the core of her heartache. She trembled in his arms, her body shaking with silent sobs, and whispered Vusi's name over and over, like it was the only thing connecting her to reality, as if saying it could somehow pull him back. Thomas did not speak. He simply held her, knowing that no words could lessen the grief. The room held its breath along with him, the silence punctuated only by Zonke's quiet sobs. When the tears finally subsided, and the stillness pressed in around them, she looked up at him with her swollen, bloodshot eyes, her soul laid bare. Thomas had been waiting— patient, silent—giving her the space she needed to open up when she was ready.

"He is gone, Thomas," she whispered, her voice broken and fragile. "He is gone, and I will never get to see him again." Her face crumpled with the threat of fresh tears, but she quickly wiped them away, too exhausted to cry anymore.

Thomas remained quiet, his presence speaking louder than any words could. She knew he was there for her, listening.

"I miss him," she said, holding back her tears. "I always have, ever since I got here. I never stopped missing him... or loving him."

"Are you talking about your old boyfriend?" he queried quietly, understanding the delicacy of the moment.

Zonke nodded slowly. "We never got a proper goodbye. How does someone go from being so full of life to... just gone? Buried in the ground like they never mattered." Her voice cracked, each word weighed down by pain and disbelief.

"I'm so sorry, Zee," Thomas whispered, his heart breaking for her. He did not know what else to say. No words could truly comfort her. But he kept her close, hoping his presence could offer some solace, even if only for a moment.

While Thomas comforted Zonke, Retha burst into the apartment, her face alight with excitement.

"My favourite human beings!" she exclaimed as she swung open the main door, blissfully unaware of the grief that hung thick in the air. Thomas quickly detached from Zonke and stood up to face Retha, knowing that the way he had been comforting Zonke might appear inappropriate in Retha's eyes. She dropped her bag onto the kitchen counter and made her way to the living room.

"Baby, guess who got promoted to Senior Associate today!" Retha's voice brimmed with pride.

She hoped for an enthusiastic response, but instead, she was met with solemn expressions. Thomas managed a strained smile as he opened his arms to embrace Retha.

"Congratulations, my love," he said, forcing warmth into his tone.

Retha tilted her head, perplexed by their reaction. "*Hawu*! I thought you both would celebrate with me. What is wrong?" Her excitement began to fade as she noticed Zonke curled up on the couch, her tear-streaked face a testament to her distress.

Zonke wiped her eyes, trying to summon a smile. "I am really happy for you," she murmured, her voice quaking with emotion.

Retha knelt beside Zonke, her earlier exuberance replaced by concern. "What is going on?" She searched Zonke's eyes, desperate for answers.

"It's just... everything feels overwhelming right now," Zonke uttered, trying to navigate her way out of explaining the source of her grief all over again.

Retha's face softened. "I understand, sweetheart. Change can often be overwhelming; you are rebuilding your life in a foreign environment. It can all feel like too much." Retha had a tendency to rush in with solutions, often before fully grasping the situation.

"Maybe we can turn this into a celebration for both of us, my promotion, your fresh start?" Retha suggested, hoping to lighten the mood.

Zonke managed a small smile, "That sounds nice."

"Great!" Retha declared, her enthusiasm reigniting. "We will make this a night to remember."

As Retha headed to the kitchen, Thomas settled back down beside Zonke. "You okay?" he asked softly, concern lining his face.

"Just need some time," she replied, leaning into him for comfort. "But I am glad Retha is happy."

"Me too," Thomas admitted, "And we will get through this together, okay?"

Zonke nodded, feeling a bit of comfort seep into her heavy heart.

\*\*\*

It was during their dinner celebration at an elegant restaurant at the V&A Waterfront that life took an unexpected turn for all of them. The atmosphere buzzed with laughter and the clinking of glasses, yet a sudden shift loomed on the horizon, unnoticed by the trio. Retha and Thomas sat side by side, their fingers intertwined, while Zonke faced them from across the table, her gaze distant and lost in thought.

As the warm glow of the restaurant enveloped them, Retha finally broke the momentary silence, her tone a mix of excitement and trepidation. "So, my promotion to Senior Associate… um, there's more to it," she hesitated, struggling to convey the drawbacks of her advancement.

Thomas smiled, though anxiety tightened in his chest at the thought of what she was about to reveal.

Retha continued, her voice dropping as she revealed the downside of her newfound success. "I will have to move to London next year. It is a fantastic opportunity, but…" Her words trailed off.

"What?" Thomas replied, a sudden sting of betrayal surging through him. "Do you understand how far away you will be from me? From us, Retha!?" His flustered tone cut through the lively atmosphere.

Zonke remained silent, her eyes darting between Retha and Thomas.

"Yes, I do. I do, baby." Retha said, trying to maintain her composure. "But think about our future. This could be a stepping stone for all of us."

Before she could elaborate, Thomas abruptly stood up, the chair scraping against the floor, and walked away from the table, leaving a palpable tension in the air.

# CHAPTER SIX

*A FLEETING MOMENT OF PASSION*

The beginning of the new year brought about changes that enveloped the trio—Zonke, Retha, and Thomas—with a heavy sense of uncertainty. Retha had spent the last two months of the previous year trying to convince Thomas that their relationship could withstand the miles between them, insisting that love, if nurtured, could bridge any distance. It had taken time, but eventually, he agreed to commit to long-distance. Yet, just as Retha found a way into Thomas's heart again, she learned she had more work to do, this time with Zonke.

Zonke's confession surfaced on a quiet evening, her voice soft yet filled with doubt. "I can't stay here without you, Retha," she reasoned when asked why she would even consider returning to Jabavu after all the progress she had made.

Retha shook her head. "No. No. You are not going back there, cuzz," she said firmly. "I don't want you to return to that toxic environment. Cape Town has been good to you, hasn't it?" Zonke's eyes drifted to the floor. "It has, but—"

"But nothing!" Retha interrupted, her tone softening as she gently lifted Zonke's chin, forcing her to look back at her.

"This is your home now. Even if I am not here, Thomas is. He is like an older brother to you, just as I am like your older sister."

Zonke let out a small, reluctant smile. It was hard to argue with Retha's logic, but the nagging pull of Jabavu still lingered in the back of her mind.

"I need you to start your studies this year," Retha continued, her words a quiet command but filled with love. "It is time to focus on you."

Zonke pondered Retha's words, realising that the new year promised an odyssey of self-discovery for her. Despite the anxiety surrounding the impending changes, including Retha's departure, she felt a growing anticipation to rewrite her story.

***

It was a week before schools reopened, and Zonke was set to begin her studies, when a fleeting moment of passion unraveled everything she had worked for—her dreams, her healing, her self-discovery—all thrown into chaos. That impulsive night had been preluded by a friendly invitation to a dinner date from Thomas.

Zonke stood by the balcony, gazing at the sunrise stretching across the ocean, a coffee mug warming her hands. She pondered the new season of her life, feeling a thrill as she considered the possibilities awaiting her return to school. She imagined the friends she would make, the fresh routine, and her renewed passion for learning. In that quiet moment, it hit her—she would finally get to be a teenager again, free from the suffocating presence of an abusive lover. Though she still missed Vusi and grieved his death, she realised how much of her youth had been lost to loving him. She had surrendered parts of herself to make their relationship work. She had burnt herself alive to keep their fire alight. The gap between them (eight years!) now seemed stark, a fledgling girl entangled with a grown man. She had fallen for Vusi before she fully blossomed into her womanhood, before she even knew who she was or who she could become. As the sun climbed higher, painting the sky in red and orange hues, she felt a deep sorrow for her younger self—a girl who had given too much too soon. Just as she began to delve deeper into her thoughts, Thomas joined her on the balcony, interrupting her inner reflections.

"Morning, Morning, Zee!" he greeted with enthusiasm.

He was dressed for work in a grey two-piece suit that flattered his body shape perfectly. Moving closer, he offered her a quick side hug.

"Good morning," Zonke replied with a smile, returning the embrace.

"I am off to work," he said, pulling back from the hug, "but I was thinking we could do dinner at a restaurant in Camps Bay tonight." He suggested casually. "You can pick the restaurant," he added.

"Okay, sure," Zonke uttered with a touch of confusion in her voice. *Why the dinner?* Sensing her hesitation, Thomas smiled. "I mean, we ought to celebrate your return to school before you officially start." He winked playfully. Zonke could not help but chuckle, sharing in his lightheartedness.

"Alright, alright, you are right. Let's celebrate!"

"Great! It's a deal, then. I will see you tonight," Thomas said as he exited the balcony.

"Bye!" Zonke called after him.

Later that night, Zonke and Thomas enjoyed dinner at a simple yet sophisticated restaurant with a stunning sea view. As they dined, Zonke indulged in nostalgia, sharing stories of Jabavu. She spoke of the warmth that enveloped her hometown, where it was not unusual to go knocking next door with an empty cup, politely asking a neighbour for sugar or fish oil when supplies ran low mid-month. She recalled the communal spirit, where greeting everyone on the street was customary, each acknowledgment a sign of mutual respect. Families did not need to send out formal invitations for their ceremonies; the sight of a tent in a yard, music spilling out into the air, was enough to draw in friends and neighbours. They knew that laughter and celebration would go with a plate of food, often filled with freshly slaughtered meat, and traditional beer to wash it down.

"Rumours spread faster than tumours," she chuckled, highlighting the tight-knit nature of her community. Despite the challenges—alcohol and drug abuse, violence, teenage pregnancy, and poverty—Zonke recognised that Jabavu held a special place in her heart, filled with cherished memories that shaped who she was.

"Do you miss it?" Thomas asked when she fell silent.

"Of course! It's home!" she replied, gripped by nostalgia. "But I like it here too. It's good for me." Her tone was calm, reflective.

"Good. That's good. I, we, like having you around," Thomas confessed, stretching out his hand to touch Zonke's. She looked up at him, and for a moment, they lost themselves in each other's eyes, a connection deepening between them. Just as their unspoken bond felt like it could transcend words, a waiter approached, interrupting their moment.

"Ma'am, your dessert," he announced, breaking the spell. Zonke and Thomas exchanged glances, both smiling as they shifted back to the present. The waiter placed a bowl of ice cream in front of Zonke.

"Thank you," she said, glancing back at Thomas, who had not ordered any dessert for himself.

"Where I come from, it is rude to eat alone while someone else is drooling over your food. Let's share?" she offered, a playful glint in her eyes.

Thomas chuckled, amused by her coaxing. "You are going to make me break my diet," he joked, then grabbed a spoon and scooped a generous portion of the ice cream.

As he brought the spoon to his lips, Zonke watched him, a smile creeping onto her face. She thought about how he scooped the ice cream the same way he had scooped her from the bitterness of her past, inviting her to savour the sweeter memories instead.

The rest of their evening at the restaurant had been blissful, and by the time they got home, laughter and joy lit up their faces. Zonke hurried to kick off the high heels that had left her feet ablaze. As she sank into the couch, Thomas poured them each a glass of wine. She winced at the pain in her feet, unused to wearing high heels for so long, especially since they were not even hers but Retha's.

"She left them behind for a reason; she doesn't need them," Thomas had said earlier, convincing her it was fine to wear them for dinner. Now, though, Zonke regretted it as her feet throbbed.

"Come on, let me massage those feet. I can tell they need it," Thomas offered, handing her the wine glass.

Zonke giggled, feeling shy. *Massages are too intimate*, she thought. "No, I will be fine, thank you," she said, taking the glass from him.

But Thomas reclined on the couch beside her, set his own glass down, and lifted her feet onto his lap. Her toes curled as he fondled them, his touch gentle, slow, and rhythmic. Zonke glanced down at her feet in his hands and let her gaze trail up to his handsome face. He seemed focused on his task but was fully aware of her lingering stare, knowing she enjoyed the warmth of his hands against her skin. A sly smile crept across his face before he met her eyes with a fierce intensity. She bit her lip, her suggestive expression stirring a primal reaction in him. Blood rushed down his underbelly, his manhood hardening with desire. Her vagina tingled, competing with her toes, and intensifying the tension between them.

He lowered his head and kissed her foot, causing her to giggle before pulling her legs back and setting them on the floor. Sensing an opportunity, he seized the moment by closing the gap between them. Their faces inched closer, breaths quickening, and soon their lips met, erasing all thoughts of anything else.

Their heightened senses and the pulse of desire pulled them down a forbidden path, one they could not resist as their erotic passion intensified.

# CHAPTER SEVEN

*THE JOYS OF WOMANHOOD*

The morning after a young woman experiences sexual intimacy following a long, unintentional celibacy, she awakens to her inner thighs singing songs of praise. Her heart dances joyfully, pumping the glow of passion to her face. Her body radiates a sensual energy, her smile betraying the heightened vibration coursing through her. The joys of womanhood!

When a young woman embraces the pleasures of her femininity, her bosom and buttocks bloom with the bliss of her newfound liberation.

Zonke, however, woke up the next morning with a body swelled with regret after her night of passion with Thomas—Thomas, who had woken up earlier than usual and hurried off to work before the sun even came up. He, too, was burdened by regret and shame. Thomas had revived the emotions and thoughts she last felt when she woke up naked in Vusi's bedroom. The only man she trusted served her a cold plate of rejection after she had opened her legs to him. *Men!* She thought bitterly, staring at the ceiling, hating herself all over again.

Her mind spiralled through memories of every moment when she had felt that agonising self-hate. Every time, it had been because of a man—her stepfather, Vusi, and now Thomas. She never expected it from him. Thomas had become a ray of sunshine in her life, along with Retha. He had embraced her with a love that made the hate once shrouding her body fall away in clumps, and now he redressed her with it.

*What is wrong with men?!* she thought, fighting against the sting of betrayal she felt in her heart.

*What is wrong with me?!*

A flame of fury ignited in every fibre of her being, burning through her confusion and hurt, leaving her seething with anger—at him, at herself, at the world that seemed to conspire against her peace.

# CHAPTER EIGHT

## SHATTERED DREAMS

It had been three months since that fleeting night of pleasure and passion between Zonke and Thomas when Retha returned home for a brief visit. In her absence, Zonke and Thomas had carried on as though nothing had ever happened. They never spoke of their affair, never hinted at the intimacy they had shared, and never came close to each other again in that way. Life went on as though the connection between them had never existed, and the betrayal of Retha lingered in the shadows, unspoken but ever-present. They simply returned to being friends, though they had emotionally drifted apart.

The following evening after their fateful night, Thomas walked in after work, holding takeaway bags from Zonke's favourite restaurant, pretending everything was fine.

"Hey, Zonke! Look what I brought you," he announced, lifting the bags with a forced enthusiasm that belied the tension between them.

Zonke looked up from the couch and feigned a smile. She had spent all day thinking about what had happened between them, bracing herself to confront him, to ask why he had left her without a word that morning, without any clarity on what they were or what their night together meant. But as she looked at him now, standing there as if nothing had changed, she decided against saying anything. Instead, she played her role of pretence in the play he had orchestrated. They sat down together in the living room, sharing the meal in silence, each pretending it was just another night, while unspoken truths saturated the space between them.

When Retha visited, she returned to the familiar comforts of home, to what she expected—her boyfriend and cousin were friends, not lovers. The atmosphere felt unchanged.

***

Everyone around Zonke, especially Retha, saw a young girl finally moving forward, her life seemingly on the right track. And for a time, Zonke herself believed it too. The light of her future seemed to glimmer brighter, and she felt certain that the shadows of her past would remain locked away, never to return. With new friendships flourishing at school and a sense of belonging among her peers, her hope for a better life was revived. But just beyond her sight, a storm brewed on the horizon.

It was while Retha was visiting that the dark clouds began to gather, threatening to turn Zonke's fragile peace into chaos. She had woken up with a queasy, vertiginous sensation that crept up slowly, beginning as a mild nausea before growing into an overwhelming urge to vomit. She barely made it to the bathroom before she emptied her stomach, just as she was preparing to leave for school. The episode left her weak and clammy. When Zonke mentioned to Retha that she was not feeling well, Retha assumed it was something minor, perhaps an upset stomach or bile. Neither of them expected the news the doctor would soon deliver.

Usually, the doctor delivered such news with a smile, starting with *congratulations!* But as he sat across from Zonke in her school uniform, Retha beside her, anxiously holding her hand, he felt awkward and sad for her. He was uncertain how to articulate the words that typically brought pride and joy to older women but now loomed as a shameful burden for a young girl, especially a school student. He glanced at Zonke, then Retha, and cleared his throat.

"So, what is wrong with my cousin, Doctor?" Retha asked, her tone a mix of impatience and politeness.

"Well, Miss Zonke is not sick, but—" he began, only to be cut off by Retha.

"Not sick? She was vomiting this morning," she interjected, her concern deepening.

Zonke sat in silence, her heart pounding painfully in her chest, feeling as if the room was spinning around her. She stared blankly at the floor, battling a rising tide of emotions—fear, shame, and confusion—swirling together like a tempest. A part of her knew what the doctor was about to say. She had spent the last few weeks denying the possibility of it, clinging to hope even as her mind wrestled with the reality of her situa*tion. My last period was in January,* she thought, panic surging through her as she counted the months. It was now April. Fear and worry had begun to creep in a few days earlier, but she quickly brushed it aside. *This has happened before.*

Before she moved to Cape Town. Before she met Thomas. Before they—

*It has happened before!* she affirmed to herself, trying to soothe her racing heart. But she had forgotten the crucial detail that had eased her anxiety back then: she was on birth control, which had significantly affected her menstrual cycle. Irregular bleeding, unexpected spotting, and even months without a period had been her norm. But that was then, and she had stopped using birth control when she ended things with Vusi and left Jabavu.

Now, the strain of her denial felt heavier than ever. With each heartbeat, the truth loomed closer. As the doctor delivered the results, Zonke found herself lost in a maze of thoughts—calculations and frantic reassurances. Beside her, Retha sat engulfed in the heaviness of the moment, her anxiety palpable as they both grappled with the shocking reality unfolding before them.

"Yes, and based on the tests we've done, I can confirm that she is not ill. What she is experiencing is actually morning sickness," the doctor explained.

Retha's expression shifted dramatically, the colour draining from her face as the realisation hit her like a slap. Her mind raced, grappling with the implications of the doctor's words. She looked at Zonke, searching for reassurance, but found only a void of uncertainty reflected back at her.

"But morning sickness is..." she faltered, struggling to comprehend what this revelation meant for her cousin's life and future.

"Miss Mashaba, your cousin is pregnant." The words lingered in the air, suffocating, as if the very atmosphere thickened with the enormity of the revelation.

Zonke's breath caught in her throat, and she finally looked up at Retha, fear shining in her eyes. Retha's mouth fell open, and for a moment, the world around them disappeared, leaving only the two of them suspended in a reality that had just shifted irrevocably.

# CHAPTER NINE

*CHAOS*

Zizipho's voice echoed in the room, cutting through the tension like a blade. "Zonke! Since when do you have a boyfriend? Why do you even have a boyfriend so soon after all that has happened? Are you not there to focus on yourself?" Her words came out fast, angry, laced with disappointment.

Retha, Thomas, and Zonke sat in strained silence around the dinner table, the phone sitting in the middle like a loaded weapon. Zizipho's voice crackled from the other end, her frustration burning through the line. From the moment the doctor shared the news of Zonke's pregnancy, Retha knew this was something she could not handle alone. After leaving the doctor's office, she had been unable to hide her fury, letting the silence between her and Zonke stretch as they drove home. The chasm between them felt vast, and she was barely holding back her anger. When they reached home, she called Zizipho immediately and, despite her rage, asked Thomas to join them at the table. *He has been taking care of her all this time*, she had reasoned, blissfully unaware of the part he played in this chaos. Now, as they all sat there, the gravity of the revelation crashing down, Thomas was just as shocked as Zizipho when Retha finally broke the news.

Zonke sat quietly, her shoulders hunched as if she wanted to disappear. Her hands fidgeted in her lap, fingers tangling and untangling in anxious motions. She could not meet anyone's eyes, least of all Retha's. The shame was too much. And Thomas? She felt his presence beside her like a load pressing down on her.

Thomas, still reeling from the revelation, shifted uncomfortably in his seat. His mind raced, the truth gnawing at him, but he kept his thoughts to himself. He could not even begin to process what all of this meant, not just for Zonke, but for him, for Retha, for their entire dynamic. The tension in the room grew with every second, unspoken accusations clinging to the walls.

"Answer me! Who is the boy?" Zizipho demanded furiously.

"Mama, I... There's—" Zonke stammered, her voice trembling, words failing her as she tried to explain the storm of emotions swirling inside her.

Tears began to roll down her cheeks, her breath hitching as she let out a quiet sob. No one moved to comfort her— neither Thomas nor Retha, and certainly not Zizipho.

Zizipho, having lost all patience and compassion, was only interested in answers now.

"How far along is she, Retha?" Zizipho's fury seemed to settle slightly as she directed her question at Retha.

"The doctor said twelve weeks now," Retha replied, "I am so sorry this has happened, Ma," she added, guilt rising within her for not protecting her cousin better.

"No, no. This is not your fault. I am sure you did not send her out to sleep around," Zizipho reassured Retha, though her anger was still palpable. "Twelve weeks…" she muttered, her voice trailing off as she pieced the timeline together. "That must have been late January. Were you in London then?" she asked, trying to make sense of it all.

"Late January, yes, I was long gone, Ma," Retha confirmed. She glanced at Zonke, then added, "That was actually before school started, so she had not met anyone from school yet."

"When she should have been focused on going back to school and changing her life, she decided it was better to run around with boys." Zizipho's voice dropped into dismay before rising sharply again. "*Sies*, Zonke!" she shouted, her words sharp with disgust and disappointment. "I am beyond disappointed, *m'tanami.* You have not changed at all, not even one bit!"

Zonke looked up, her tears blurring her vision as Retha's piercing gaze bore into her, forcing her to blink back even more tears. Her mind hopscotched back to all the times she had been sexually intimate with Vusi, both before and during her time on contraceptives. So many times! So many moments, some now just faint memories, others blurry and darkened, and yet she had never fallen pregnant. But with Thomas, a single moment of weakness, and now she was carrying his child. The irony felt like a cruel twist of fate, and a sharp loathing for Thomas began to surface. *This is a shame! I must be cursed. It would have been better if I had gotten pregnant by my own boyfriend, not by betraying my cousin so openly.* Her guilt-ridden thoughts tormented her, only to be abruptly interrupted by Retha.

"Why are you quiet? Your mother is talking to you," Retha snapped, her patience wearing thin. Zonke's tears only heightened her frustration. "Crying won't change anything," she added coldly.

All the while, Thomas sat quietly, unmoving, like an outsider. Zonke could not bring herself to look at him, nor could she confess that it was him who had done this to her. Together, they had tried to forget that night, to bury the truth. But her body remembered every vivid detail of their affair; it had captured evidence of that night, evidence that now grew inside her, shaking her to the core, promising to bloat her belly and expose the truth.

*This secret will shatter our world*, Zonke thought to herself, struggling to bury the truth deep inside.

"Why is she crying? If I were there, I would slap those tears off her face," Zizipho yelled over the phone, echoing Retha's harshness.

"Speak up!" Retha demanded, her voice sharp and unrelenting. "We want to know the name of the boy who did this to you. Is he from this complex? Where did you meet him?"

Zonke flinched at Retha's tone, her body trembling under the pressure. Slowly, her gaze shifted towards Thomas, her eyes wide and pleading. Her silent desperation was clear—she needed him to save her, to shield her from the storm raging around her. But Thomas froze, the fear tightening around him like a noose, choking his voice. Retha's eyes followed Zonke's gaze, landing on Thomas. The silence between the two, the way their gazes met, triggered something deep within her. Retha was sharp— a lawyer, skilled at picking up unspoken truths, reading between the lines, and unearthing lies. Her heart pounded against her chest as the horrifying realisation started to settle in. *It can't be,* she thought, her breath growing shallow as her mind unraveled the terrible possibility.

"Thomas?" she whispered, her voice barely audible, trembling with disbelief. Her heart raced, each beat more painful than the last.

Thomas could not look back at her, his eyes darted around the room as if looking for a way to escape, his shame overwhelming him.

"Thomas," she repeated, louder this time, her voice cracking as the truth dawned on her.

Thomas finally spoke, his voice shaking, tears welling in his eyes. "I am sorry... I am so sorry, Retha."

Retha let out a disbelieving chuckle, her gaze drifting away from them both. The sound was sharp and bitter, like glass shattering.

Throughout the tensely whispered confession, Zizipho had remained quiet, hoping her wordless presence would pressure Zonke to speak. But nothing could have prepared her for what came next.

Still chuckling, Retha's laughter twisted into something darker, a maddened rage simmering beneath the surface. She grabbed the phone, her hand trembling, and addressed Zizipho with venom in her voice. "Ma, this whore you call your child, this whore slept with my boyfriend. She slept with my boyfriend!" Tears now streamed down her face, her words a ragged hiss, raw with betrayal. An unfamiliar fury burned through her heart.

"*Haibo!* Zonke?" Zizipho gasped as the shocking revelation sank in.

Retha's eyes locked onto Zonke, now filled with a hatred so fierce it was almost blinding. Without warning, she shot up from her chair, moving with such terrifying speed that Thomas barely had time to react.

She charged at Zonke like a bullet, her rage unleashed, and in that moment, nothing could stop the calamity that followed…

# CHAPTER TEN

*EYE OF THE STORM*

It was not the storm that had been brewing for months that shattered familial bonds, destroyed a promising relationship, and upended a young girl's life; it was the aftermath of it, the wreckage left in its wake. There was no moving forward from what had happened, no way to rewrite the past. In a single, irreversible moment, both the past and future had been obliterated. The present was now an agonising nightmare, echoing the burden of what could never be undone.

Retha had not been thinking when she lashed out, her actions driven by blind, destructive rage born from betrayal. But now, behind cold prison bars, reality gripped her with icy hands. The fury had left her, replaced by a sickening clarity. A once-successful lawyer, now a murderer—a prisoner, all because of an affair. Guilt engulfed her, and loneliness crept into her heart like a slow, suffocating fog. She had been there for everyone, always the strong one, the reliable one. But now, when she needed someone, anyone, to stand by her, she found herself utterly alone. No one was there. Not Thomas, not Zizipho, and certainly not Zonke. No one.

In the lonely, dark silence of the prison, her muddled mind replayed the moment her world fell apart—how she discovered her boyfriend's betrayal, murdered her cousin, and in a matter of moments, shattered everything she had built. Her fortress of success crumbled in what felt like the blink of an eye.

*She remembered springing from her chair, propelled by a fury that felt otherworldly, as she launched herself at Zonke. Grabbing the vase from the dining table, she hurled it with all her might, the porcelain shattering against Zonke's skull. A sharp shard of glass sliced into her flesh, and time seemed to freeze in that violent, devastating moment. Blood spurted from Zonke's head, splattering the floor in a dark crimson arc.*

*Zonke tried to utter something in vain, her voice a mere whisper against the chaos. "I am sorry, Retha," she gasped, blood gushing from her mouth, the words barely forming as her strength waned.*

*Retha stood over her, frozen in time, unable to move, speak, scream, or cry. The gravity of her actions pressed down on her like a heavy mantle. Thomas watched in horror from where he sat, trembling, paralysed by the reality unfolding before him. He knew he could do nothing to erase the nightmare. The world around them fell into a dead silence as Zonke took her last breath.*

*With shaking hands, Thomas picked up the phone, whispering into it in despair, "She is dead. She is dead. She is dead!" He repeated the words like a mantra as if uttering them could summon Zonke's spirit back to life.*

*Zizipho's deafening screams swallowed up the silence, drowning out the echoes of the tragedy...*

# About The Author

Okuhle Esethu, legally known as Lindokuhle Esethu Hlatshwayo, is a visionary creative writer and editor with a rich background in literature, film, and drama.

She holds a Bachelor of Arts degree in Communications and Media and English Literature from the University of Johannesburg, along with an Honours degree in English Literature with a Scriptwriting minor from the University of Cape Town.

As an accomplished author, she has written and published ten books, each one a testament to her exceptional talent and dedication to her craft.

Armed with a deep understanding of storytelling conventions, she fearlessly breaks the rules to ignite creativity in her writing.

www.ingramcontent.com/pod-product-compliance
Lightning Source LLC
Chambersburg PA
CBHW031850170626
46807CB00004B/1664